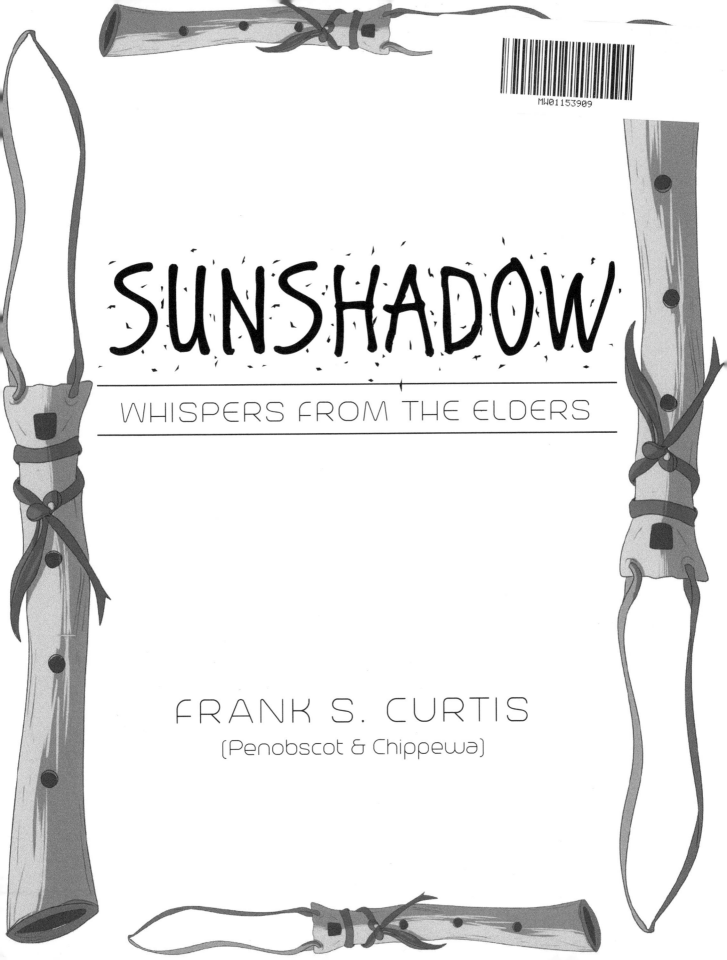

SUNSHADOW

WHISPERS FROM THE ELDERS

FRANK S. CURTIS

(Penobscot & Chippewa)

PAGE PUBLISHING, INC.
New York, NY

First originally published by Page Publishing, Inc. 2017

ISBN 978-1-68348-724-1 (Paperback)
ISBN 978-1-68348-725-8 (Digital)

Printed in the United States of America

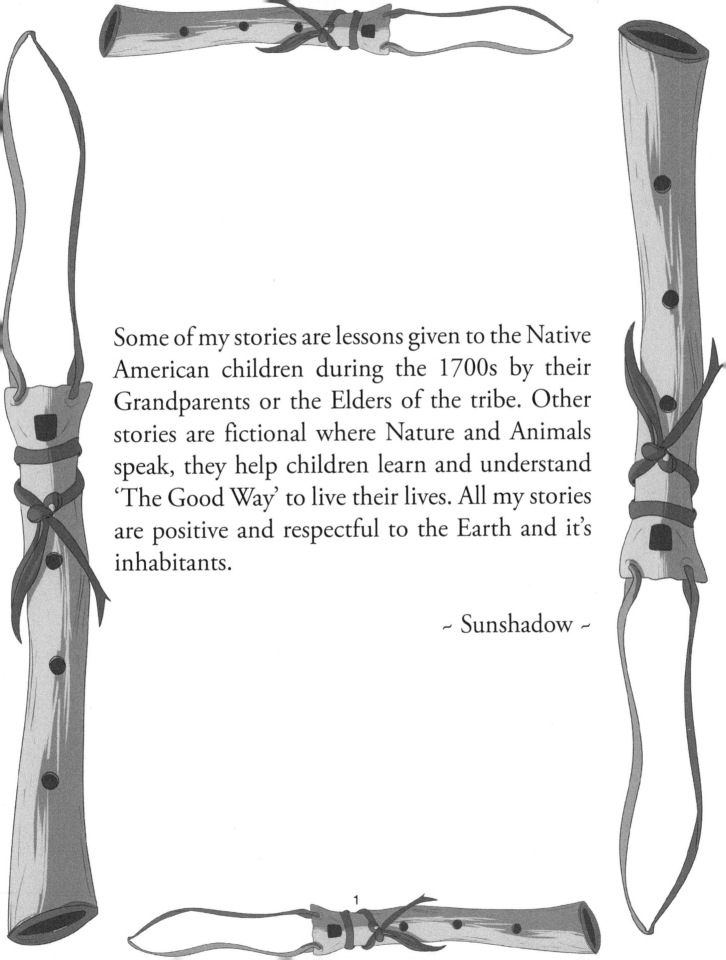

Some of my stories are lessons given to the Native American children during the 1700s by their Grandparents or the Elders of the tribe. Other stories are fictional where Nature and Animals speak, they help children learn and understand 'The Good Way' to live their lives. All my stories are positive and respectful to the Earth and it's inhabitants.

~ Sunshadow ~

HOW SUNSHADOW WAS GIFTED HIS NAME

In the land of the Great Basin, where Nevada, Arizona and Utah meet, there is a place now called Kodachrome Basin. In this place, the rocks and cliffs grow high and rugged. On the west side is a spot called Shakespeare's Arch. The rising sun hits a small hole in the rock wall, and a beam of light moves along the desert below.

While hiking this area, my wife Ellen and I found ourselves at the end of the beam. This bit of time must have been sent by the Creator. At that moment, I did not question the reason.

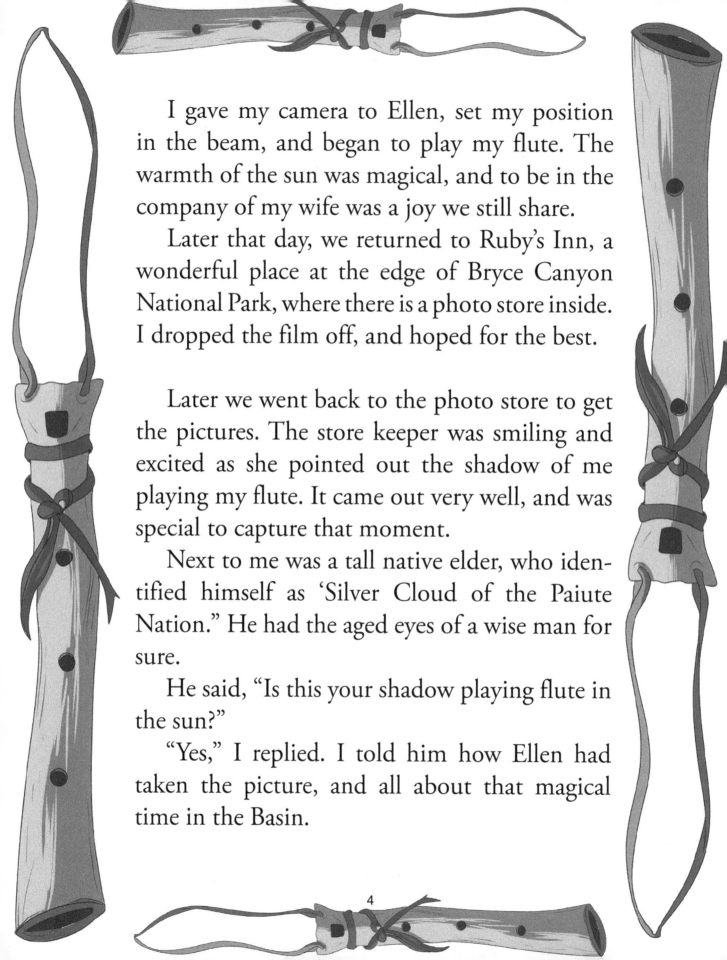

I gave my camera to Ellen, set my position in the beam, and began to play my flute. The warmth of the sun was magical, and to be in the company of my wife was a joy we still share.

Later that day, we returned to Ruby's Inn, a wonderful place at the edge of Bryce Canyon National Park, where there is a photo store inside. I dropped the film off, and hoped for the best.

Later we went back to the photo store to get the pictures. The store keeper was smiling and excited as she pointed out the shadow of me playing my flute. It came out very well, and was special to capture that moment.

Next to me was a tall native elder, who identified himself as 'Silver Cloud of the Paiute Nation." He had the aged eyes of a wise man for sure.

He said, "Is this your shadow playing flute in the sun?"

"Yes," I replied. I told him how Ellen had taken the picture, and all about that magical time in the Basin.

Silver Cloud said, "You must be a good flute player. It is a good sunshadow. The Creator was pleased by your song."

Silver Cloud fell silent for a moment then asked, "What is your native name?"

I told him about my grandmother being of the Penobscot Tribe in Maine and my grandfather's family being of Chippewa blood.

"They have both crossed over. I have their spirit, but not a native name."

Silver Cloud smiled and said, "If they could see this photo, they would agree with me. I will call you Sunshadow, is that name good with you?"

I responded, "I am honored, thank you."

It was a good day; I believe that it has led me to this day.

Safe journey, Sunshadow

Note, the term "Safe Journey" is used by a number of Native Americans

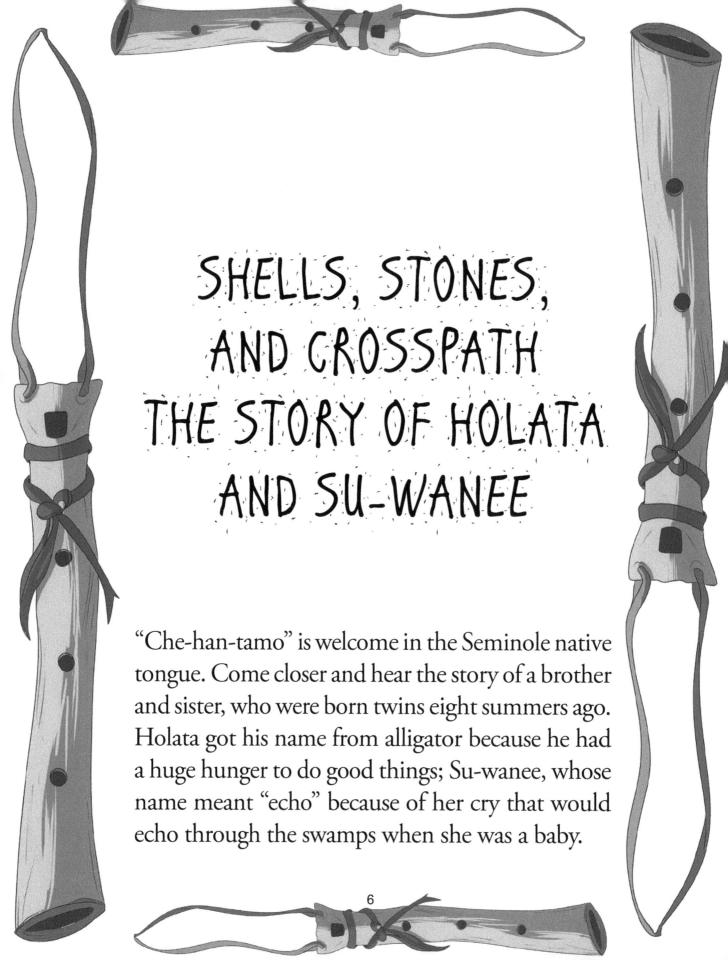

SHELLS, STONES, AND CROSSPATH THE STORY OF HOLATA AND SU-WANEE

"Che-han-tamo" is welcome in the Seminole native tongue. Come closer and hear the story of a brother and sister, who were born twins eight summers ago. Holata got his name from alligator because he had a huge hunger to do good things; Su-wanee, whose name meant "echo" because of her cry that would echo through the swamps when she was a baby.

Their home was in the Seminole Nation, near a small river that made its way to the sea, where the sun sets. Holata and Su-wanee were strong and wise. Each day, they would walk a bumpy path form their village to the sea. It was a beautiful sight to see, and their favorite things were shells and stones. Su-wanee would run to find her shells while Holata would get stones at the end of the river before the sea swallowed all of them. They both spent time picking their colors and shapes before going home.

Each time Holata and Su-wanee returned home, they would unload the packs of shells and stones. They set about putting their collections in order. Holata would place the small stones around their dwelling, and the large stones were placed around the fire area in the center of the village.

Su-wanee put her shells around the inside of their home. The small shells with natural holes in them were laced on thin strips of deer hide so they could be worn around the neck. She gifted these to all her family and friends.

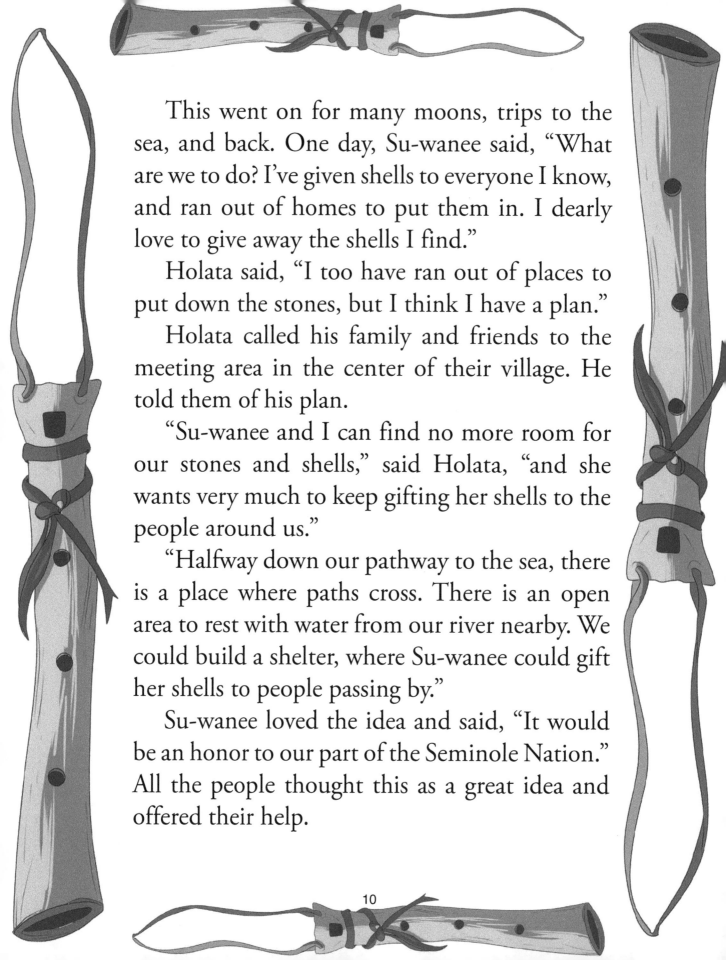

This went on for many moons, trips to the sea, and back. One day, Su-wanee said, "What are we to do? I've given shells to everyone I know, and ran out of homes to put them in. I dearly love to give away the shells I find."

Holata said, "I too have ran out of places to put down the stones, but I think I have a plan."

Holata called his family and friends to the meeting area in the center of their village. He told them of his plan.

"Su-wanee and I can find no more room for our stones and shells," said Holata, "and she wants very much to keep gifting her shells to the people around us."

"Halfway down our pathway to the sea, there is a place where paths cross. There is an open area to rest with water from our river nearby. We could build a shelter, where Su-wanee could gift her shells to people passing by."

Su-wanee loved the idea and said, "It would be an honor to our part of the Seminole Nation." All the people thought this as a great idea and offered their help.

When Holata and Su-wanee got to the place where paths cross, they found it worn and bumpy from walkers and horses.

Holata said, "I will bring flat stones to this place, and make the path solid for walkers and even for horses." As Holata and friends gathered stones, Su-wanee and the family worked on the shelter, a table for her shells, and places for people passing by to sit and talk. This labor of love took many days to be finished. It was a wonderful place to rest, trade, and meet new people.

Holata was very busy putting stones down on the paths. He made the path two arrows wide in all directions. People could pass without bumping; even a man walking his horse had room.

Each person, meeting another, would tell the story of Crosspath. Other villages would help by adding stones. Soon, the solid path reached all nearby villages.

Su-wanee was busy collecting shells to give to the newcomers on the pathway. People from all around brought her shells, some to trade and some as gifts from friends.

Everyone was proud to know Holata and Su-wanee. Crosspath became a meeting place for trade, making friends, and resting. Seminole Chiefs, and other great leaders, met for important decisions that were made to help the Seminole people.

All this started because Holata and Su-wanee were generous and willing to share the things they loved.

Thank you, Mother Earth.

LITTLE OWL AND FATHER'S CEDAR FLUTE

Little Owl was ten summers old. Grandfather gifted him that name because his eyes were open with wonder for everything he saw.

Little Owl lived with his parents in an Abenaki Village on the edge of the Saco River. Their Wigwam was on a hill in a beautiful valley with the great White Mountains behind them.

This story begins on the day when Little Owl discovered a beautiful cedar flute beneath some blankets in the corner of the Wigwam.

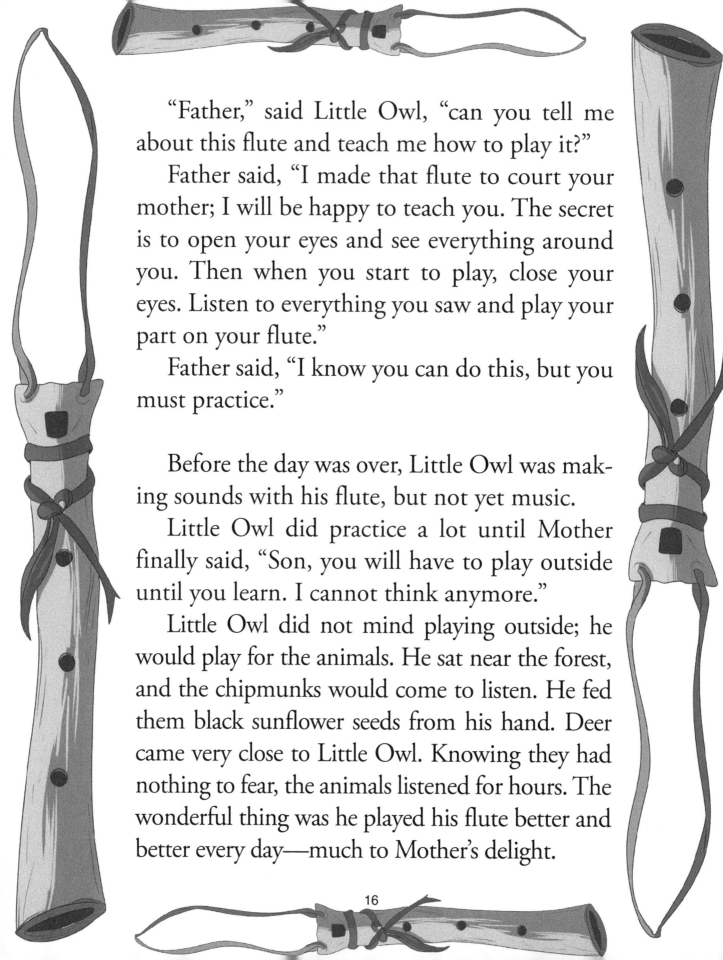

"Father," said Little Owl, "can you tell me about this flute and teach me how to play it?"

Father said, "I made that flute to court your mother; I will be happy to teach you. The secret is to open your eyes and see everything around you. Then when you start to play, close your eyes. Listen to everything you saw and play your part on your flute."

Father said, "I know you can do this, but you must practice."

Before the day was over, Little Owl was making sounds with his flute, but not yet music.

Little Owl did practice a lot until Mother finally said, "Son, you will have to play outside until you learn. I cannot think anymore."

Little Owl did not mind playing outside; he would play for the animals. He sat near the forest, and the chipmunks would come to listen. He fed them black sunflower seeds from his hand. Deer came very close to Little Owl. Knowing they had nothing to fear, the animals listened for hours. The wonderful thing was he played his flute better and better every day—much to Mother's delight.

One day, Little Owl looked behind him and saw many people from the village. They listened quietly to the music. Everyone told Little Owl how proud they were because he was playing his flute so well.

Little Owl made a plan. He asked his Mother and Father if he could hike up the Great White Mountain. He would play for all the animals and people he met along the way. His parents thought this was a very good plan. Mother made a beautiful bag to carry his flute. Father packed him food, a warm coat, and flint for a fire.

The next day, father walked with Little Owl to the base of the Mountain. The weather was clear. Father said, "The Mountain is a very dangerous place. If the weather gets bad, I want you to turn around. You will be safe; your Flute will comfort you. The animals and stars will show you the way. I will listen for the flute on your return. Safe journey my son."

Little Owl was off on his quest . . .

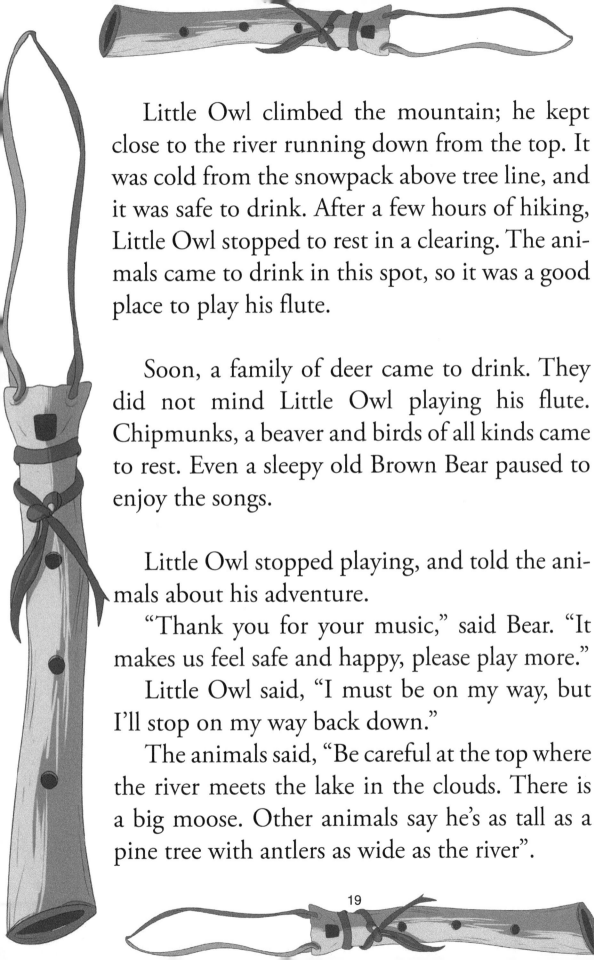

Little Owl climbed the mountain; he kept close to the river running down from the top. It was cold from the snowpack above tree line, and it was safe to drink. After a few hours of hiking, Little Owl stopped to rest in a clearing. The animals came to drink in this spot, so it was a good place to play his flute.

Soon, a family of deer came to drink. They did not mind Little Owl playing his flute. Chipmunks, a beaver and birds of all kinds came to rest. Even a sleepy old Brown Bear paused to enjoy the songs.

Little Owl stopped playing, and told the animals about his adventure.

"Thank you for your music," said Bear. "It makes us feel safe and happy, please play more."

Little Owl said, "I must be on my way, but I'll stop on my way back down."

The animals said, "Be careful at the top where the river meets the lake in the clouds. There is a big moose. Other animals say he's as tall as a pine tree with antlers as wide as the river".

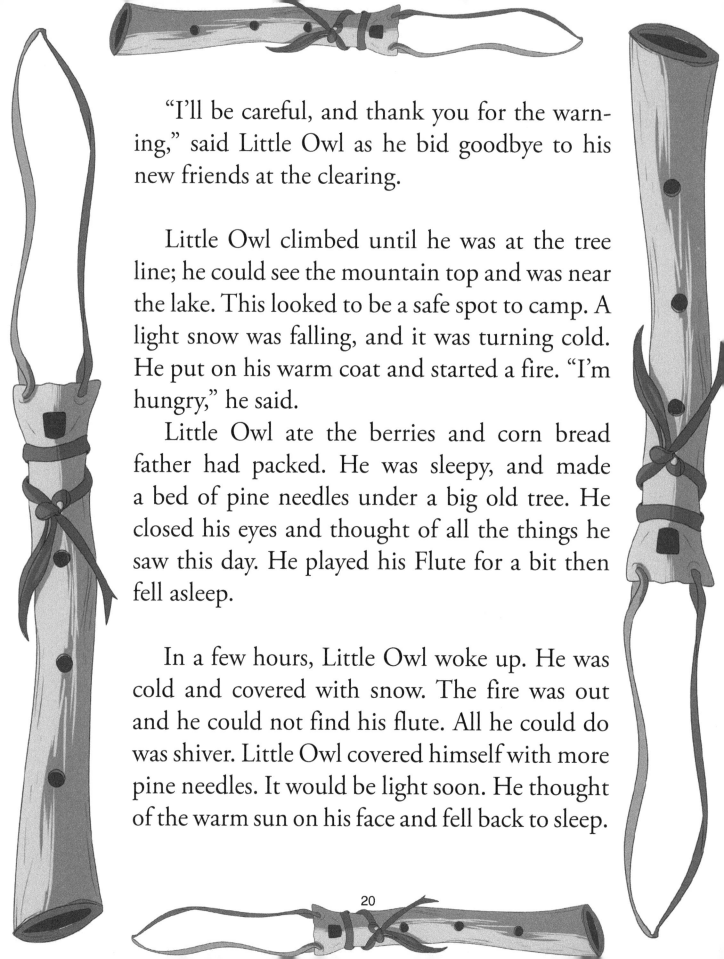

"I'll be careful, and thank you for the warning," said Little Owl as he bid goodbye to his new friends at the clearing.

Little Owl climbed until he was at the tree line; he could see the mountain top and was near the lake. This looked to be a safe spot to camp. A light snow was falling, and it was turning cold. He put on his warm coat and started a fire. "I'm hungry," he said.

Little Owl ate the berries and corn bread father had packed. He was sleepy, and made a bed of pine needles under a big old tree. He closed his eyes and thought of all the things he saw this day. He played his Flute for a bit then fell asleep.

In a few hours, Little Owl woke up. He was cold and covered with snow. The fire was out and he could not find his flute. All he could do was shiver. Little Owl covered himself with more pine needles. It would be light soon. He thought of the warm sun on his face and fell back to sleep.

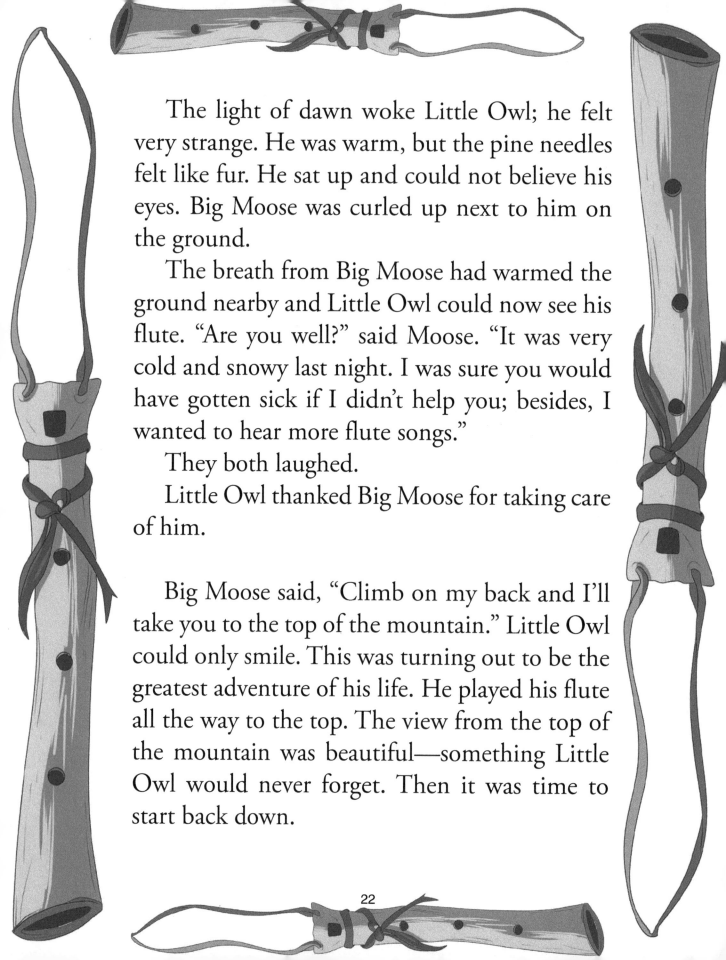

The light of dawn woke Little Owl; he felt very strange. He was warm, but the pine needles felt like fur. He sat up and could not believe his eyes. Big Moose was curled up next to him on the ground.

The breath from Big Moose had warmed the ground nearby and Little Owl could now see his flute. "Are you well?" said Moose. "It was very cold and snowy last night. I was sure you would have gotten sick if I didn't help you; besides, I wanted to hear more flute songs."

They both laughed.

Little Owl thanked Big Moose for taking care of him.

Big Moose said, "Climb on my back and I'll take you to the top of the mountain." Little Owl could only smile. This was turning out to be the greatest adventure of his life. He played his flute all the way to the top. The view from the top of the mountain was beautiful—something Little Owl would never forget. Then it was time to start back down.

Big Moose again let Little Owl ride on his back down the mountain. When they got to the clearing by the river, his animal friends were waiting. They could not believe their eyes, Little Owl riding on the back of Big Moose.

"This is our friend," said Little Owl. "I am sure he saved my life on top of the mountain. You have no reason to fear him."

It was a wonderful lesson to learn. Little Owl played his flute at the clearing. He saw Mother and Father coming. He jumped to his feet hugged them and told them his incredible story. Little Owl thanked everyone for keeping him safe and being his friend—there was such love around him. This was a good day for Little Owl, but an even better day for all who enjoyed the songs from Father's Cedar flute.

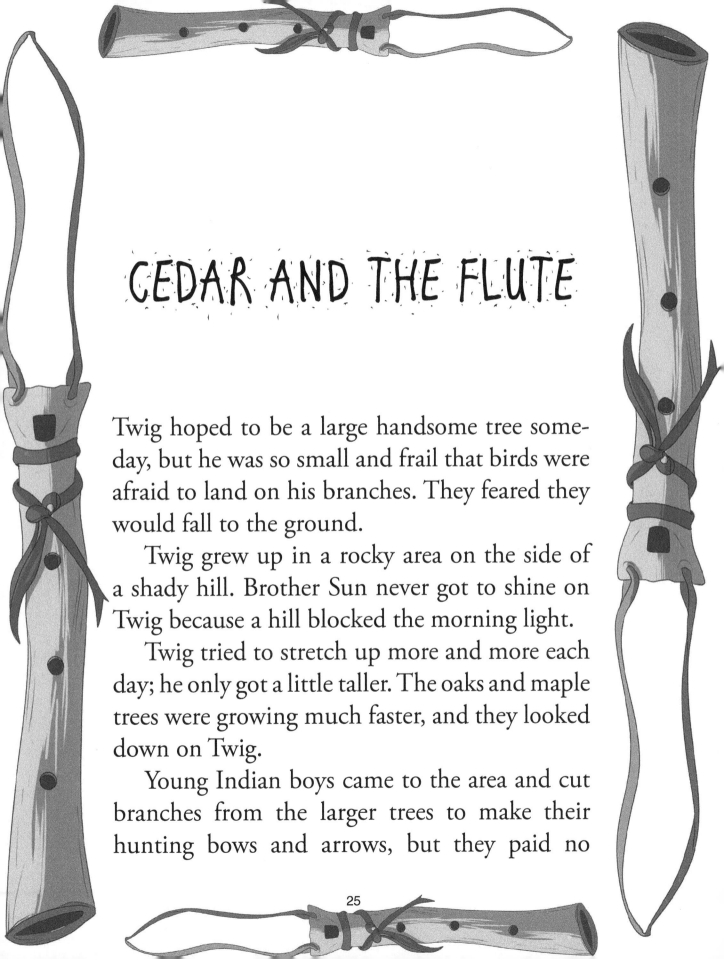

CEDAR AND THE FLUTE

Twig hoped to be a large handsome tree some-day, but he was so small and frail that birds were afraid to land on his branches. They feared they would fall to the ground.

Twig grew up in a rocky area on the side of a shady hill. Brother Sun never got to shine on Twig because a hill blocked the morning light.

Twig tried to stretch up more and more each day; he only got a little taller. The oaks and maple trees were growing much faster, and they looked down on Twig.

Young Indian boys came to the area and cut branches from the larger trees to make their hunting bows and arrows, but they paid no

attention to little Twig. Birds made nests in the bigger trees, and baby birds learned to fly from their branches, but Twig was never considered.

Twig never stopped trying to grow. He kept pushing up, and moving side to side. He got a little bigger each day. He was straight and tall, but not tall enough to see Brother Sun.

One morning, Twig woke up to a very bright light in his eyes. He looked behind him and saw a wonderful sight, it was his shadow! Twig turned back and felt the warmth that Brother Sun gave his branches. Twig felt himself getting stronger.

In the days and moons that followed, Twig became a beautiful Cedar tree. His rich brown colors and wonderful smell was something all Indians looked for.

The young Indian Braves said, "Cedar, when you get bigger, we can use your branches for lodge poles and arrows. Your shavings will start our fires, and the smell of your wood will bring peace and happiness to our people".

Days passed, a young man came to sit under Cedar's branches, he looked sad. Cedar called the man Dark Cloud, because it reminded Cedar of the days before he felt the warmth of Brother Sun on his bark. Brother Sun made Cedar happy and he hoped it would make this young man happy. Cedar said to the man, "What makes you so sad Dark Cloud? What is in your dreams?"

Dark Cloud said, "In my village, there is a maiden that I care for very much, but she will not look my way. Each day she watches the boys playing hunting games. She seems to be impressed by their games of strength."

Cedar thought for a while and said, "Dark Cloud, why don't you cut off one of my branches and carve it into a whistle to get her attention."

Dark Cloud liked this idea very much. He carefully cut a branch from Cedar.

Dark Cloud carved and trimmed the branch for a time. He cut holes to make sounds. He found it easy to carve the soft wood.

Dark Cloud liked the sound of the first holes so much that he made more holes in the branch—each with a different tone.

Cedar could not believe the beautiful sound coming from the whistle. Cedar said, "That branch deserves a much better name. I will call it a flute, a happy song stick."

Dark Cloud played his Flute and made up wonderful songs. Tears fell from Cedar's leaves. These were tears of joy because something from his branch could sound so beautiful. All the trees around smiled, and Brother Sun made the area warm and happy.

Dark Cloud thanked Cedar for the gift. Cedar said, "Go now and play your best songs for the maiden! I'm sure she will fall in love with you now."

A few moons later, Cedar was awakened by the sounds of a large group of people around his gathering place.

All the people were listening to Dark Cloud telling the story of how Cedar grew from a tiny Twig to the majestic tree of now. He told of Cedar's gifts to help the villagers, and the story of the flute that brought people to this gathering.

Dark Cloud and his maiden, Sunshine, were being married under the watchful shade of Cedar. The sound of Flute was heard all around, and everyone was happy. This day was full of love.

Thank you,
Brother Sun

THE STORY OF NEHIAH (BOY HUNTER) (PRONOUNCED NEE-HI-AH)

The man called Black Feather was known as a great hunter and gatherer of food for his family and village. He was also known for his patch of corn for bread and greens used to sweeten the stew in the boiling pots.

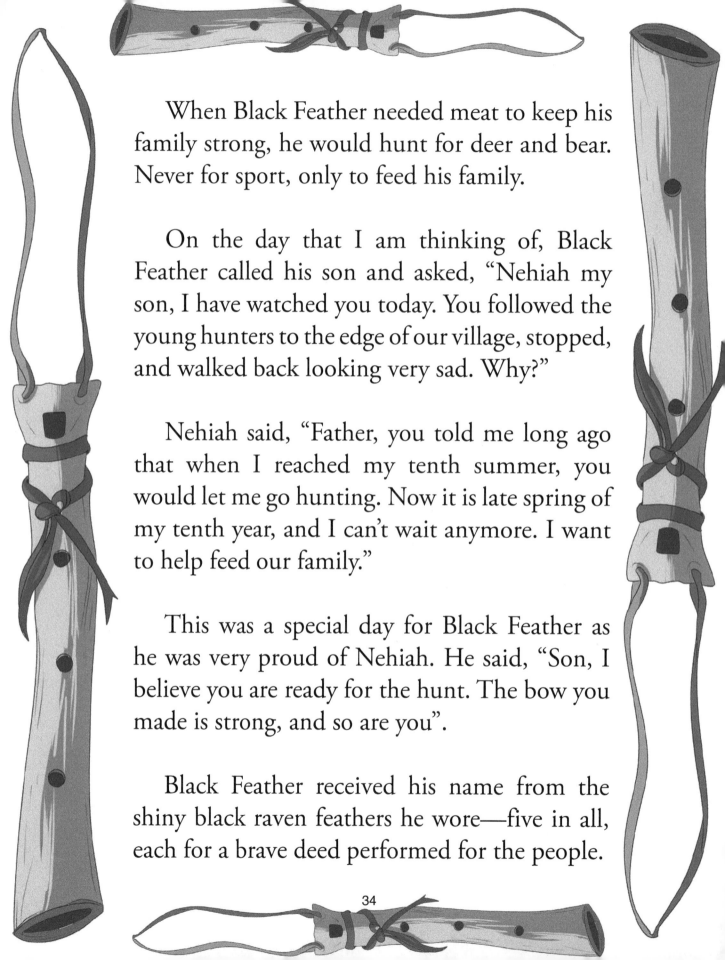

When Black Feather needed meat to keep his family strong, he would hunt for deer and bear. Never for sport, only to feed his family.

On the day that I am thinking of, Black Feather called his son and asked, "Nehiah my son, I have watched you today. You followed the young hunters to the edge of our village, stopped, and walked back looking very sad. Why?"

Nehiah said, "Father, you told me long ago that when I reached my tenth summer, you would let me go hunting. Now it is late spring of my tenth year, and I can't wait anymore. I want to help feed our family."

This was a special day for Black Feather as he was very proud of Nehiah. He said, "Son, I believe you are ready for the hunt. The bow you made is strong, and so are you".

Black Feather received his name from the shiny black raven feathers he wore—five in all, each for a brave deed performed for the people.

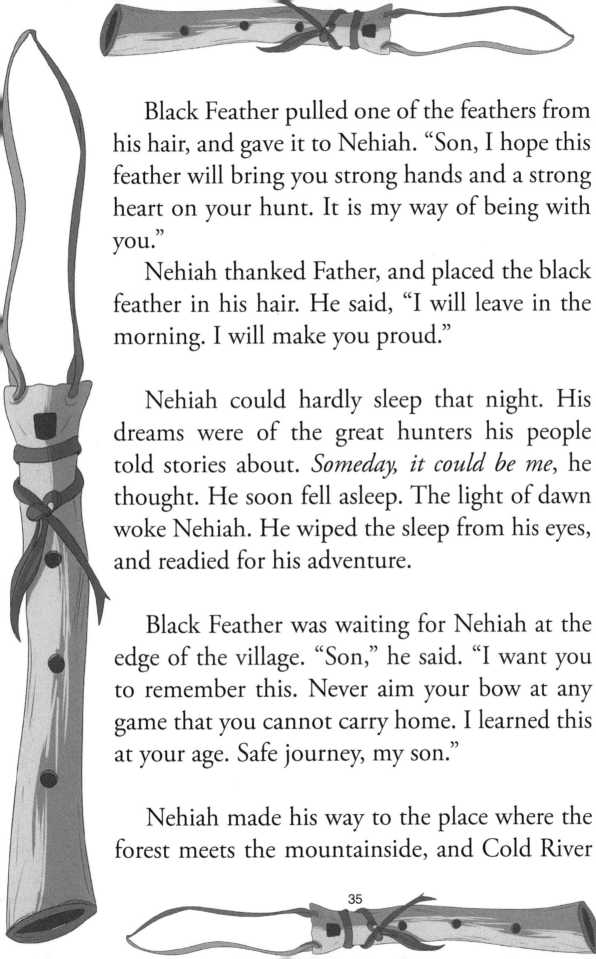

Black Feather pulled one of the feathers from his hair, and gave it to Nehiah. "Son, I hope this feather will bring you strong hands and a strong heart on your hunt. It is my way of being with you."

Nehiah thanked Father, and placed the black feather in his hair. He said, "I will leave in the morning. I will make you proud."

Nehiah could hardly sleep that night. His dreams were of the great hunters his people told stories about. *Someday, it could be me*, he thought. He soon fell asleep. The light of dawn woke Nehiah. He wiped the sleep from his eyes, and readied for his adventure.

Black Feather was waiting for Nehiah at the edge of the village. "Son," he said. "I want you to remember this. Never aim your bow at any game that you cannot carry home. I learned this at your age. Safe journey, my son."

Nehiah made his way to the place where the forest meets the mountainside, and Cold River runs swiftly. Nehiah's Father said it would be a good place to find game. Nehiah searched for wild turkey with no success. He tried to catch a rabbit, but the rabbit was much too quick.

Nehiah sat next to the river thinking out loud, "How can I come home with empty hands?" He watched a salmon swim past. Nehiah thought, *If I could catch a large fish that would be good, and would please Father.*

Nehiah reached for the fish. He lost his footing and tumbled into Cold River. He was a good swimmer, but the river was much too swift. Nehiah could hardly stay above water. He bumped hard into rocks for what seemed to be a very long time.

Nehiah finally gained his balance when the river became shallow. He looked ahead and saw a very large figure. As he floated closer, he saw a full grown Grizzly Bear fishing for salmon. Two other bears were nearby.

Nehiah thought, *"How can I get away? I know they see me."* He tried to swim to shore, but his strength was gone. Cold River swept Nehiah right next to the Grizzly. Nehiah could do nothing, but to stop. The bear's paws were enormous, bigger than Nehiah's head. Grizzly reached for Nehiah, but instead of hurting the boy, the bear lifted Nehiah up in his arms and carried him to shore. He placed Nehiah gently on the ground.

Grizzly said to the boy, "Are you alright boy cub?"

Nehiah was stunned and could only stare into the eyes of the giant bear. They were joined by the other two bears. "Don't worry little Black Feather," said Grizzly. "I mean you no harm and neither do my sons." Nehiah could not believe his ears. "How did you know the name Black Feather? That is my father's name."

"Many summers ago," said Grizzly, "a young hunter came to this forest. I was fishing in the river. I looked up, and the hunter had his bow aimed at my chest. That hunter looked around,

saw my two young cubs near me, and slowly lowered his bow and arrow. That hunter wore the same Black Raven feather that I saw in your hair as you bobbed up and down in Cold River. I knew you were his boy cub."

"Each time your father hunts. He visits us and we catch salmon for him."

"It seems," Grizzly said, "the fish that we caught this day, was you." They all laughed and Grizzly gifted the largest salmon caught that day to Nehiah.

Grizzly said, "Go home now and tell your father of this day. Also tell him how you are now part of our Bear Clan."

Nehiah thought this was a good day to make friends and a better day to be alive.

"I am sure Father will be proud of me." His heart was full of love.

"Safe Journey, Nehiah."

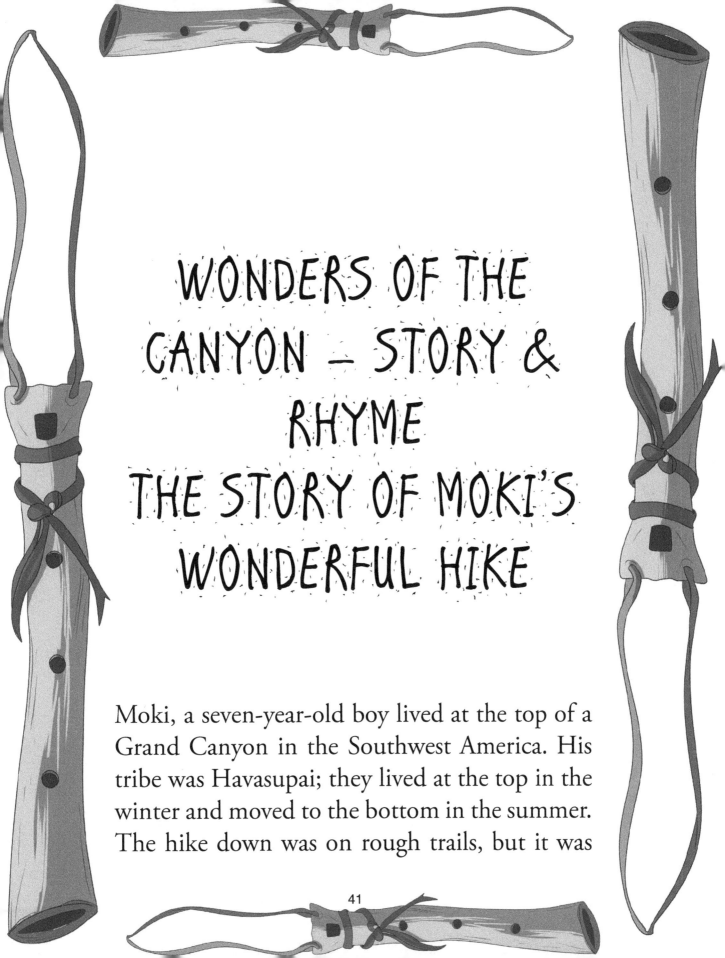

WONDERS OF THE CANYON – STORY & RHYME
THE STORY OF MOKI'S WONDERFUL HIKE

Moki, a seven-year-old boy lived at the top of a Grand Canyon in the Southwest America. His tribe was Havasupai; they lived at the top in the winter and moved to the bottom in the summer. The hike down was on rough trails, but it was

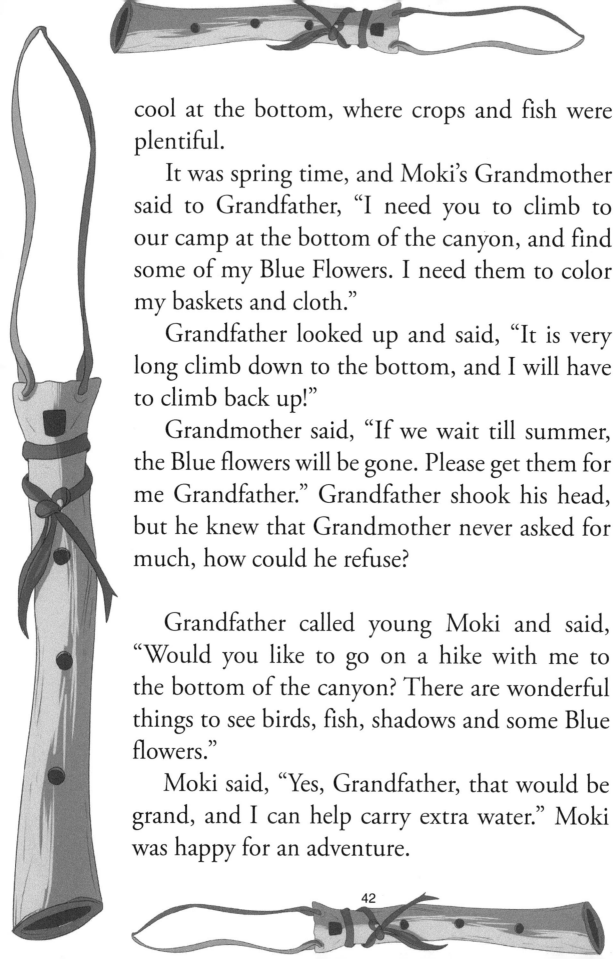

cool at the bottom, where crops and fish were plentiful.

It was spring time, and Moki's Grandmother said to Grandfather, "I need you to climb to our camp at the bottom of the canyon, and find some of my Blue Flowers. I need them to color my baskets and cloth."

Grandfather looked up and said, "It is very long climb down to the bottom, and I will have to climb back up!"

Grandmother said, "If we wait till summer, the Blue flowers will be gone. Please get them for me Grandfather." Grandfather shook his head, but he knew that Grandmother never asked for much, how could he refuse?

Grandfather called young Moki and said, "Would you like to go on a hike with me to the bottom of the canyon? There are wonderful things to see birds, fish, shadows and some Blue flowers."

Moki said, "Yes, Grandfather, that would be grand, and I can help carry extra water." Moki was happy for an adventure.

They started down the canyon trail in the distance; they heard Grandmother yell, "Don't forget my blue flowers."

Moki started singing, "I'm going to see the canyon. I'm going to have a good time. Grandfather and I will make a story and sing it as a fun rhyme."

They sang the song and made up words all the way down the Canyon. They were at the bottom in no time.

THE WONDER CANYON RHYME A SONG AND POEM BY FRANK SUNSHADOW CURTIS

Verse 1:

I'm going to see the Canyon,
Grandfather said he'd take me.
We'll walk about a half a day,
There's wonders that I must see.

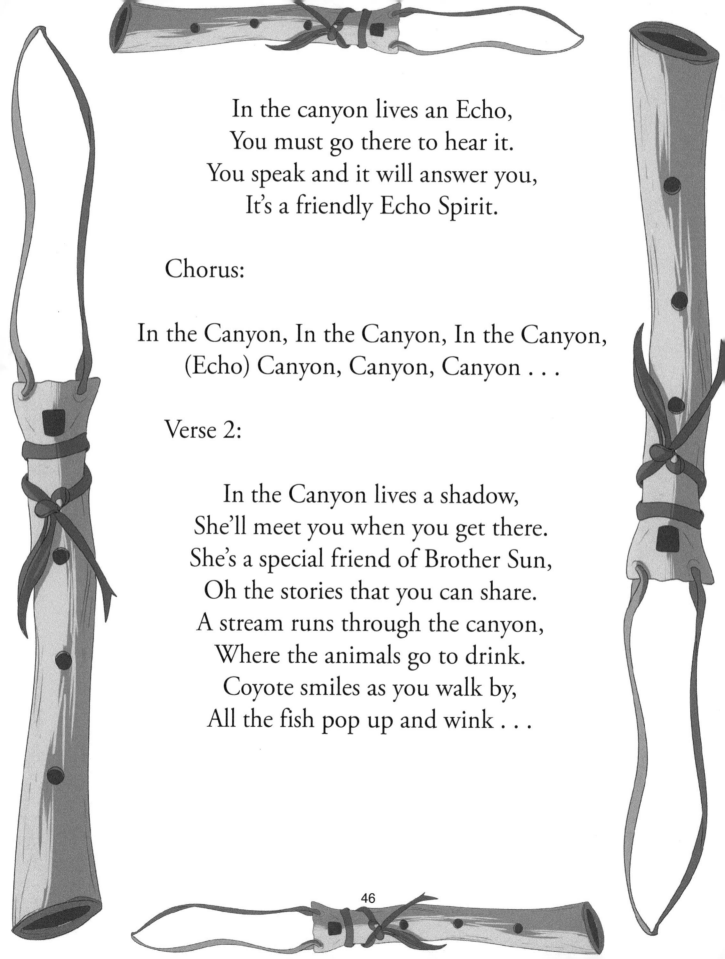

In the canyon lives an Echo,
You must go there to hear it.
You speak and it will answer you,
It's a friendly Echo Spirit.

Chorus:

In the Canyon, In the Canyon, In the Canyon,
(Echo) Canyon, Canyon, Canyon . . .

Verse 2:

In the Canyon lives a shadow,
She'll meet you when you get there.
She's a special friend of Brother Sun,
Oh the stories that you can share.
A stream runs through the canyon,
Where the animals go to drink.
Coyote smiles as you walk by,
All the fish pop up and wink . . .

Chorus:

In the Canyon, In the Canyon, In the Canyon,
(Echo) Canyon, Canyon, Canyon . . .

Verse 3:

The Canyon walls are very high,
Dressed in colors, Red and Brown.
And Eagle Soars across the Sky,
He sings as he swoops down.
I duck and fall down to the ground,
Grandfather laughs out loud!
That's Eagles way to welcome you,
You should be very proud . . .

Chorus:

In the Canyon, In the Canyon, In the Canyon,
(Echo) Canyon, Canyon, Canyon . . .

Verse 4:

Well now it's time for us to go,
We'll come another day,
It's time to share with all our friends,
The lessons learned today
About the fish that winked at us,
And birds that flew away
The Shadow and the Echo,
And walls that seem to say (pause)
(Spoken) "Safe Journey, Friends."

Chorus:

From the Canyon, From the
Canyon,From the Canyon
(Echo) Canyon, Canyon, Canyon,
Canyon, Canyon …

The End

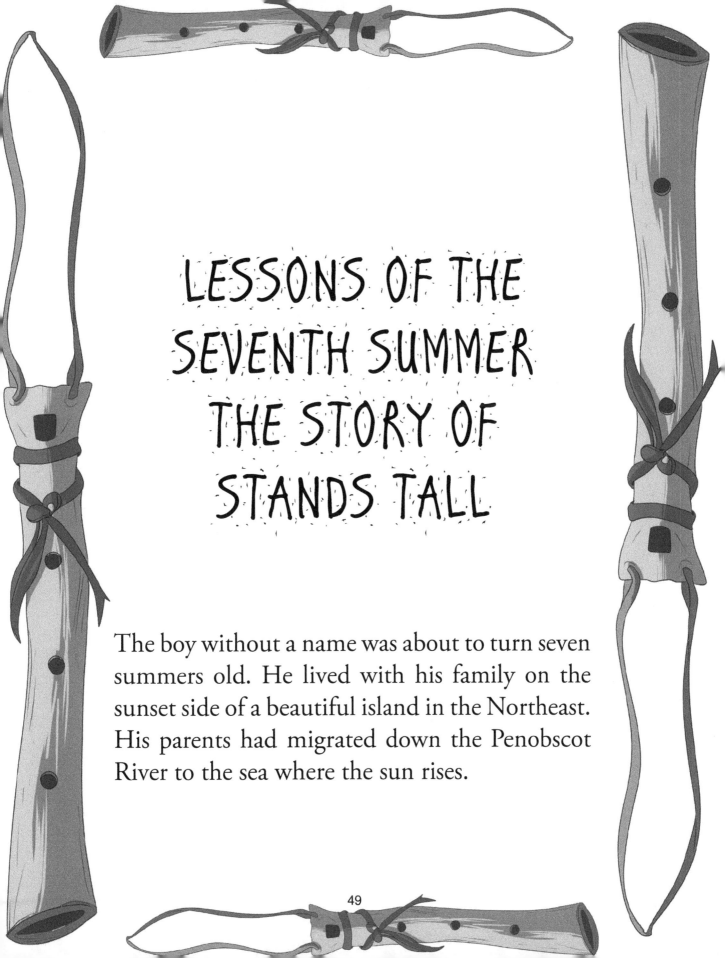

LESSONS OF THE SEVENTH SUMMER THE STORY OF STANDS TALL

The boy without a name was about to turn seven summers old. He lived with his family on the sunset side of a beautiful island in the Northeast. His parents had migrated down the Penobscot River to the sea where the sun rises.

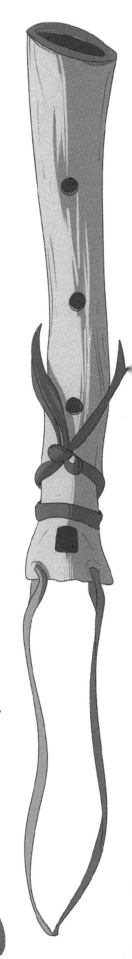

His tribe was Penobscot, part of the Wabanaki Nation. They were called the "people of the dawn."

This was an important time in the boy's life; he was to be tested by Grandfather to become a young man. Grandfather was still in the old home to the west, so the boy's father sent word by the trappers to get Grandfather to come to the Island.

In most tribal villages, the Grandparents teach the children as most parents were busy in the fields, or hunting to feed their families. Grandparents taught the history and laws of the tribe using their wisdom to test children on their life passages.

Soon after the snow and ice melted around the island, Grandfather arrived. He was a tall man dressed in buckskin from head to toe. He looked very wise indeed. He had a long crooked staff and a shorter stick with feathers used to point the good way. Grandfather wore eagle feathers in his hair. He must have done good things for his people.

Grandfather looked at the boy and said, "You cannot be the boy I am here to teach, you are much too tall." Part of Grandfather duties was to name the boy.

"I know what your name is to be," said Grandfather. "You will be Stands Tall. That is your name!"

Stands Tall was very happy to finally have his Indian name. He thanked Grandfather.

"Don't thank me yet my son, you still need to be tested." Grandfather chuckled.

"I am ready as soon as you are rested." Stands Tall laughed.

After Grandfather rested, he and Stands Tall walked to the far side of the village. Grandfather said, "Tell me of the seven directions we must travel in our lives!"

Stands Tall thought about the four colors mother had sewn into his coat. The colors black, white, red, and yellow were to tell directions.

"Grandfather," said Stands Tall. "I know the answer. West is where the thunder beings live; it brings us rain and that is the color black. North

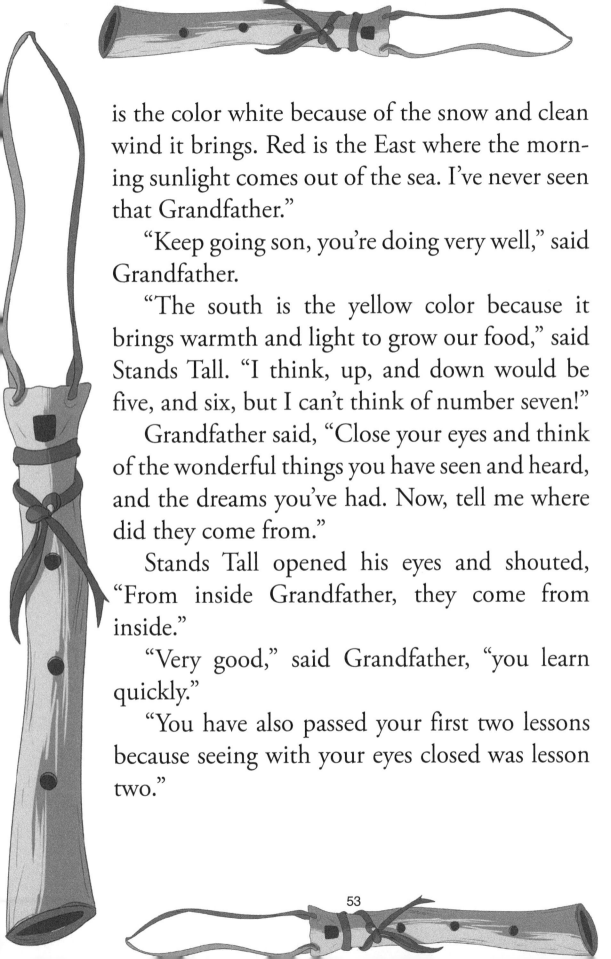

is the color white because of the snow and clean wind it brings. Red is the East where the morning sunlight comes out of the sea. I've never seen that Grandfather."

"Keep going son, you're doing very well," said Grandfather.

"The south is the yellow color because it brings warmth and light to grow our food," said Stands Tall. "I think, up, and down would be five, and six, but I can't think of number seven!"

Grandfather said, "Close your eyes and think of the wonderful things you have seen and heard, and the dreams you've had. Now, tell me where did they come from."

Stands Tall opened his eyes and shouted, "From inside Grandfather, they come from inside."

"Very good," said Grandfather, "you learn quickly."

"You have also passed your first two lessons because seeing with your eyes closed was lesson two."

"Lesson three is protecting your family, keeping them safe, warm, and fed," said Grandfather. "This becomes easier as you grow."

"Lesson four is being kind to nature and Mother Earth. Never hunt for sport; respect the animal that gives his life to keep your family fed and clothed."

"Lesson five is being respectful to others, your family, your tribe, and all those you meet on the path of life."

"Lesson six, you must keep the Great Spirit in your heart. Treat others in a good way, and live your life the good way."

"Thank you, Grandfather," said Stands Tall. "Is that all I need to know?"

"No, my son, but you must use all these things to finish your seventh and final lesson," said Grandfather.

Grandfather said, "Tomorrow you will pack for a long climb up the mountain to the East.

You told me that you've never seen the sun rise out of the sea; you will get to see that in your final lesson. Now, go and rest for your journey."

In the morning, Stands Tall packed a warm coat, some food, a small mirror, a gift from the trappers, and a three-note whistle he had carved from bone. It made the sound of the eagle. When Stands Tall was ready to leave the village, all the tribe wished him well. His parents said they would be waiting with food when he returned. Grandfather told him of things to watch for and use the mirror to signal when he reached the top. Grandfather handed Stands Tall a flint and some wool to start a fire. "It may get cold tonight."

Stands Tall hiked all day. The trail was well marked by others of his tribe. He played notes on his whistle, listened to bird songs, ate berries, and drank from fresh water streams on the way. It was a very good day; he was too excited to be tired.

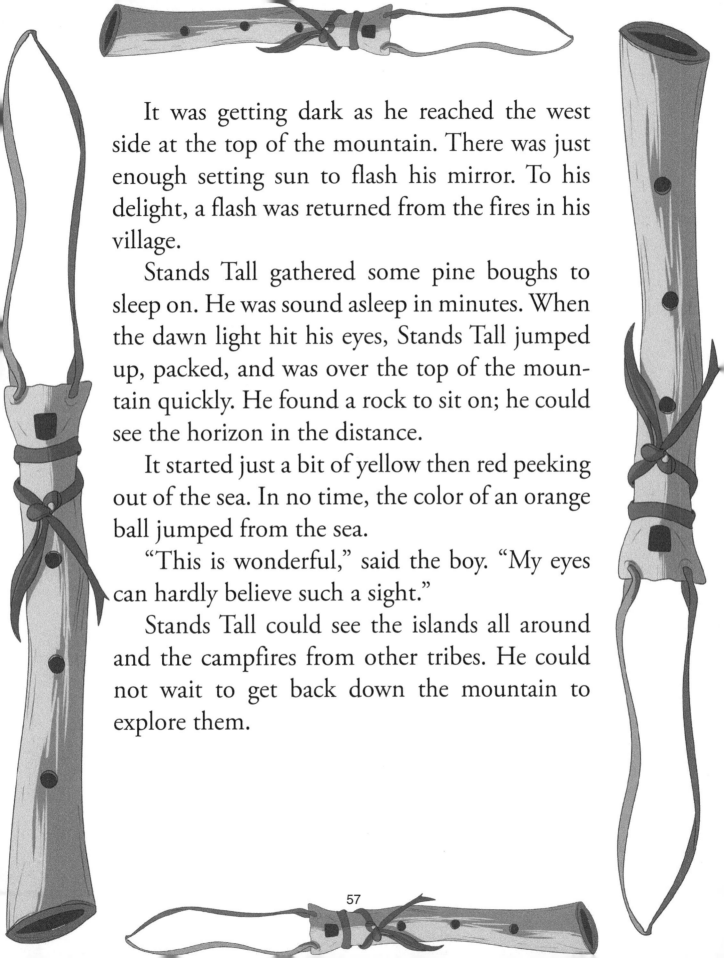

It was getting dark as he reached the west side at the top of the mountain. There was just enough setting sun to flash his mirror. To his delight, a flash was returned from the fires in his village.

Stands Tall gathered some pine boughs to sleep on. He was sound asleep in minutes. When the dawn light hit his eyes, Stands Tall jumped up, packed, and was over the top of the mountain quickly. He found a rock to sit on; he could see the horizon in the distance.

It started just a bit of yellow then red peeking out of the sea. In no time, the color of an orange ball jumped from the sea.

"This is wonderful," said the boy. "My eyes can hardly believe such a sight."

Stands Tall could see the islands all around and the campfires from other tribes. He could not wait to get back down the mountain to explore them.

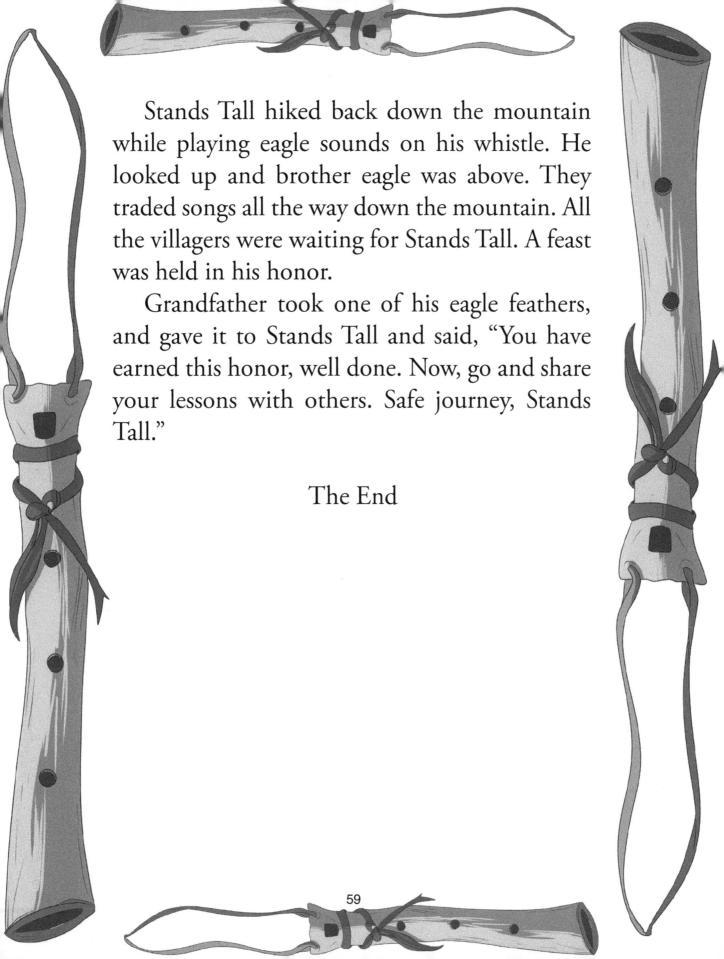

Stands Tall hiked back down the mountain while playing eagle sounds on his whistle. He looked up and brother eagle was above. They traded songs all the way down the mountain. All the villagers were waiting for Stands Tall. A feast was held in his honor.

Grandfather took one of his eagle feathers, and gave it to Stands Tall and said, "You have earned this honor, well done. Now, go and share your lessons with others. Safe journey, Stands Tall."

The End

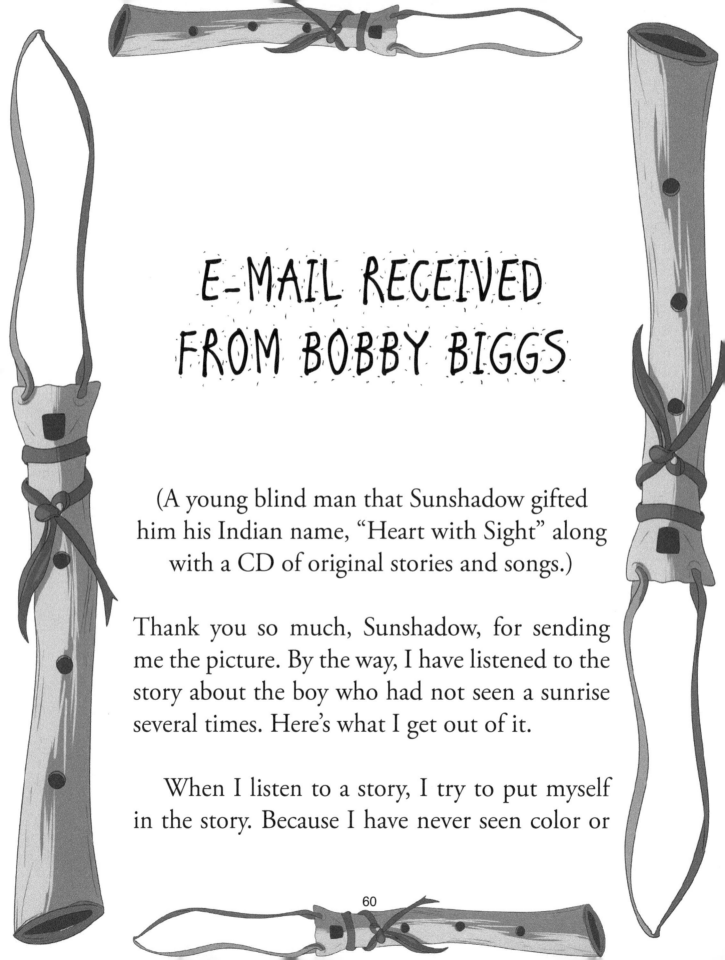

E-MAIL RECEIVED FROM BOBBY BIGGS

(A young blind man that Sunshadow gifted him his Indian name, "Heart with Sight" along with a CD of original stories and songs.)

Thank you so much, Sunshadow, for sending me the picture. By the way, I have listened to the story about the boy who had not seen a sunrise several times. Here's what I get out of it.

When I listen to a story, I try to put myself in the story. Because I have never seen color or objects or anything like that, it's hard to imagine what those things look like visually.

I have light perception and can see a little bit of shadow, but unless I know what that shadow is I can't tell what it is.

I could see myself in the story with Stands Tall. After Stands Tall talks with Grandfather Eagle and gets ready to rest, I can see myself asking him a question, "How do I keep the Great Spirit in my heart?"

I can hear him telling me that to keep Great Spirit in my heart. I should think of Him often, and talk with him like a friends talks with another friend.

I see myself walking with Stands Tall up the mountain. I imagine what his three note whistle sounds like as Stands Tall plays music.

Perhaps he and I talk. He tells me about what the birds look like and the clouds. The next day as we sit on a rock, he tells me what it looks like when the sun rises. I can see a dim light, but it grows brighter and brighter as time goes by.

Stand Tall tells me about the campfires from the other tribes that he sees. He tells me of other villages that he sees, and what the sun looks like when it is rising out of the sea.

Soon, we start to feel some heat as the day grows warmer, and we head back down the mountain.

It is truly an awesome story; probably my favorite story. I also like the story of Nehiah (I don't know how to spell his name) and the bear clan. I like the song about the canyon as well.

Thank you so much for everything, my brother. Love you also and peace and blessings be with you always.

"Heart with Sight"

Frank Sunshadow Curtis and Bobby
Heart with Sight Biggs at
Peace Tree Trading Post – Brooksville, FL

Native Flutes by Odell Borg ~ High
Spirits Flutes ~ Patagonia, AZ

ABOUT THE AUTHOR

Frank Sunshadow Curtis is a descendant of the Penobscot & Chippewa tribes in the Northeastern United States. He and his wife, Ellen, and their dog, Jake, now live in Citrus Springs, Florida, near the Nature Coast. His many talents include

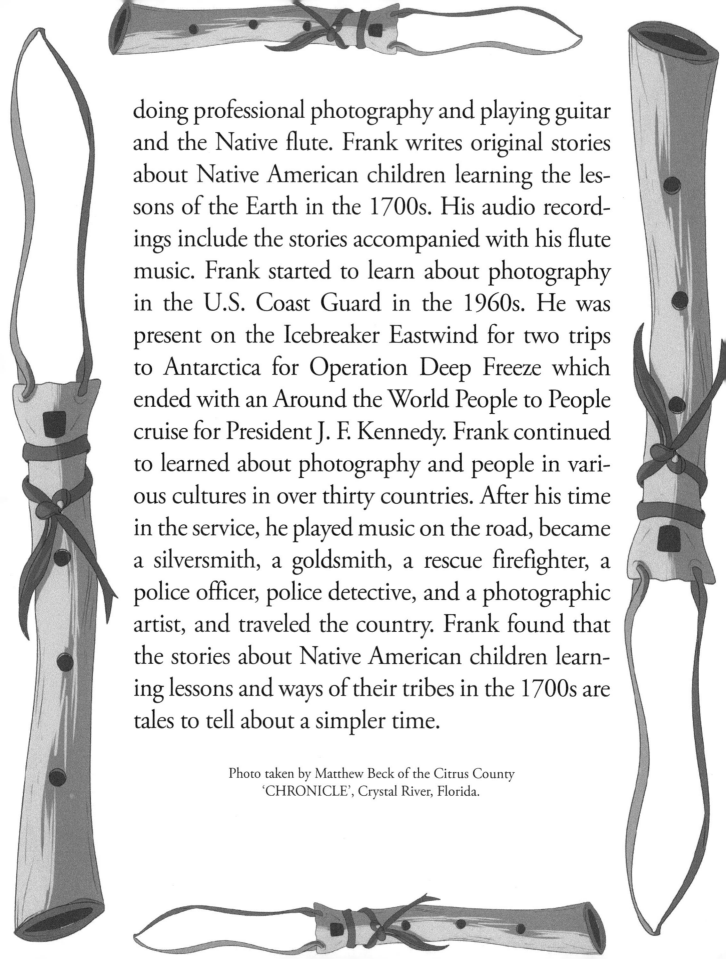

doing professional photography and playing guitar and the Native flute. Frank writes original stories about Native American children learning the lessons of the Earth in the 1700s. His audio recordings include the stories accompanied with his flute music. Frank started to learn about photography in the U.S. Coast Guard in the 1960s. He was present on the Icebreaker Eastwind for two trips to Antarctica for Operation Deep Freeze which ended with an Around the World People to People cruise for President J. F. Kennedy. Frank continued to learned about photography and people in various cultures in over thirty countries. After his time in the service, he played music on the road, became a silversmith, a goldsmith, a rescue firefighter, a police officer, police detective, and a photographic artist, and traveled the country. Frank found that the stories about Native American children learning lessons and ways of their tribes in the 1700s are tales to tell about a simpler time.

Photo taken by Matthew Beck of the Citrus County 'CHRONICLE', Crystal River, Florida.

CPSIA information can be obtained
at www.ICGtesting.com
Printed in the USA
BVHW060110230922
647537BV00001B/3

9 781683 487241